MEG and the PIRATE

for Vahmsi
in loving memory of his
grandmother, Helen Nicoll

MEG and the PIRATE

Jan Pieńkowski
and David Walser

PUFFIN BOOKS

Meg packed
her cauldron

It was a crash landing

Meg
made
a
spell

Rubies Pearls
Silver Spoons
Pieces of Eight
and Gold
Doubloons

Meg and Mog flew home